Maria Claret
THE CHOCOLATE RABBIT

BARRON'S
Woodbury, N.Y. / London / Toronto / Sydney

This is the story of Bertie Rabbit. He was a very special rabbit and it is thanks to him that there are chocolate rabbits in the shops every Easter.

Bertie had two sisters, Polly and Patty.
Every day they complained loudly,
"must we go to school?"
But Mother Rabbit wanted
them to be very wise and
she made them go. She
cooked their breakfast,
cleaned their ears and
combed their silky fur
and whiskers and sent
them off with their lunch
boxes.

Bertie's father was a fine artist.
He earned enough to keep his family
by painting Easter eggs. He used many
colors and many patterns. He painted eggs
blue, or pink, or pink with blue stripes.
He decorated them with tiny flowers and
sometimes with shining stars, or even with
wavy colored lines. He was very clever.

Every year Father Rabbit set aside a little of his hard-earned money until he could announce proudly, "We're going to have our photograph taken."

While Father Rabbit spent his days painting eggs, Mother Rabbit looked after the house and made sure Bertie and his sisters went out to collect fine fresh eggs.

The young rabbits enjoyed taking their baskets into the countryside, but Bertie often ran off to play with his friends – and he ate every carrot he could find.

Best of all, Bertie liked to go off on his own.
He would wander away
and forget all about
his sisters and about
collecting eggs.

Polly and Patty returned with their baskets
full of eggs and the latest joke they had
heard in the hen run,
such as:
Cook, cook,
there are spots
on this chicken.
That's all right,
it's only chicken pox!

One day, Bertie Rabbit had collected
some particularly fine eggs. "Hello,"
said the mice twins who were sitting
sunning themselves. Bertie stopped
to talk to them, leaving his egg basket
balanced on a stone . . . .

Crash! The basket fell over, tumbling the eggs onto the ground.

"Oh dear!" said Bertie trying to scoop them up.

"What shall I do?" wailed Bertie,
running to his sisters.

"Cheer up, Bertie," said Polly,
"you can have some of mine.
Mother will never know."

That night Mother Rabbit was so pleased with her children that she decided to make a chocolate cake. After carrots, this was their favorite food.

She set her alarm clock and settled down to sleep.

Brrr! Brrr! rang the alarm and Mother Rabbit got up to prepare the chocolate. When it was ready, she put the saucepan on one side to cool and crept back to bed.

"What a treat for my family," she thought, "and what a surprise!"

"Yummy! Yummy!" said little Bertie who was awakened by the lovely smell of chocolate.

He leaped out of bed and ran downstairs.

Bertie climbed on a stool, "just to look," he said. Then he put one little paw into the saucepan, "just to taste." Then the stool fell over . . . .

Goodness gracious! Bertie was covered all
over in chocolate. His cries awakened
the family who came running to see what
had happened.

They stood around speechless until, suddenly,
Father Rabbit shouted: "I've got an idea . . .
a marvelous idea! Why hasn't anyone thought
of it before?"

"Stay absolutely still young Bertie; don't
move a whisker."

Father Rabbit quickly got his tools and a piece of wood and started to carve. Soon he had shaped the wood so that it looked exactly like poor little Bertie, all covered in chocolate.

Mother Rabbit prepared more delicious
chocolate. Then she poured it into the
rabbit-shaped mould Father had made
from his little wooden rabbit.

While the chocolate was setting, Mother Rabbit turned to Bertie, "Off you go and wash away every bit of chocolate. I want to see my own rabbit again!"

At last the family settled down to breakfast, chattering excitedly. "We've seen the first chocolate rabbit," chanted Polly and Patty.

From that day many, many chocolate rabbits
appeared in shop windows and many, many
of them were made by the Rabbit family.

At Easter time chocolate rabbits even appeared sitting among Easter eggs on very special cakes.

And who do you think delivered all those chocolate rabbits? Why, little Bertie of course with his own yellow cart. And he never dropped a single one!